For Alison and Nick

ORCHARD BOOKS
96 Leonard Street, London EC2A 4RH
Orchard Books Australia
14 Mars Road, Lane Cove, NSW 2066
ISBN 1 85213 255 8 (hardback)
ISBN 1 85213 500 X (paperback)
First published in Great Britain 1990
First paperback publication 1993
Text and illustrations © Catherine Anholt 1990
A CIP catalogue record for this book is available from the British Library
Printed in Belgium

Catherine Anholt

Good Days

Bad Days

ORCHARD BOOKS

In our family

we have

good days

bad days

happy days

sad days

work days

play days

home days

away days

sunny days

snowy days

rainy days

blowy days

healthy days

sick days

slow days

quick days

school days

Sundays

dull days

fun days .

Every day's a different day

but the best day follows yesterday –

today!